When Someone You Love Has AIDS!

Written by **Phyllis M. Causey**

When Someone You Love Has AIDS

ISBN: 978-0-9834137-1-4

Copyright ©Phyllis M. Causey, 2011

phylliscausey@hotmail.com

Published by Causey Publishing

Printed in the United States of America. All rights reserved under International Copyright Law. Contents and/or cover may not be reproduced in whole or in part in any form without the express written consent of the publisher.

NOTICE OF DISCLAIMER: The material contained is fictional and not based on any real persons though they may be similar.

Author's Words

This story is fictional in content; however, my personal experience touched me forever and I want to share my story with others who may be suffering also.

My brother, Kenneth, died in 1985 of this tragic disease. I know the fear and the love, and how it becomes difficult as you watch your loved one suffer. The family suffers and people around you are affected by the fear.

I know that today there are medications and a lot more hope. My story ends with hope for Harold and for Mattie. Their shared experience will give each other strength.

If you have comments, suggestions, or questions, please contact me at phylliscausey@hotmail.com.

Thank you for your support. I pray that we will keep love in our hearts and in our lives.

Phyllis M. Causey

The Diagnosis

Harold Wright waited in the doctor's private office. He was waiting for Dr. Canty to tell him why he was feeling so tired and so bad. He had been having nights of chills and fever and he'd wake up drenched in sweat. Dr. Canty had been doing a series of tests and now he had some results to discuss with Harold.

"Harold," Dr. Canty came into the office. He closed the door. The look on his face was grim. He sat down at his desk and looked intently at the folder he was holding. "I am the bearer of some very bad news." He looked at Harold as if he was going to cry.

Harold was silent and still. His heart started to pound.

"Harold, some of the tests came back positive." The doctor sighed heavily. His eyes were watery. "The ones for HIV/AIDS are positive. You are HIV positive"

Harold sat motionless. He was sweating profusely. His mind was spinning. "Are you sure?" He could barely get the words out.

"I'm sure." They looked at each other. "I'm sorry, Harold. Its times like these that make me wish I had chosen another line of work. I'm just...so sorry."

Harold felt a lump in his throat. Tears were rolling down his face. "Does this mean I am going to die?"

Dr. Canty looked away. "So far we have not found a cure."

"Oh God! I'm going to die. I'M GOING TO DIE!"

Dr. Canty walked over to Harold and put his arm around him. "Harold, I want you to come to the treatment center. There's a lot of research going on there. Of course, it's all experimental right now. We haven't found any definite treatment for it yet, but we're doing everything in our power to find a way to fight this thing. You've got to help, too. If you give in, it's certain nothing is going to save you. You have to deal with it. I'll be here anytime you need me. I wish I could tell you something better... but right now, I can't."

Harold wiped his eyes and blew his nose. "I don't know what to do. I'm thirty years old and my life is over. How long, Dr. Canty?"

"It's hard to say, Harold. It depends on how hard you fight it. It depends on how strong you can be! There are cases where patients live up to five years after being diagnosed. It mainly just depends on the person. You do not have AIDS, so you have time. A person who is HIV positive can live a longer time when they take good care of themselves."

"Harold let out a sigh. "Well,...I ..." He didn't know what to say. He pulled some more tissues out of the box on the desk. "I better go now." He studied the doctor's face for a moment, and then he stood up. "I have to go."

"If you need me, Harold...anytime." Dr. Canty's eyes were spilling over. "I'll be here."

Harold paused at the door, but he didn't turn around. "Yeah,..thanks!" He left.

The drive home was a blur. Was he dreaming? Having a nightmare, maybe. It sure would be nice to wake up! He walked up the stairs to his apartment. His roommate, Paul, was in the kitchen when Harold came in.

"Who's there?" Paul yelled from the kitchen. Harold sat down on the sofa. That was as far as he could go. He was totally exhausted!
"It's me." He lay down. The picture in his head was haunting. There he was... he and Sam. The rag was tied around Harold's arm... they were helping each other...

"Damn!" He hit the sofa with his fist. "God! Please help me! I'm going to die! Why Lord? Why me? I don't want to die. I'm so scared. Oh, MY God. Help me." He closed his eyes. Maybe if he went to sleep, he would wake up and find that this shit wasn't really happening. He was so tired.

Sam came out of the kitchen. "Are you talking to yourself?"

His eyes widened when he looked at Harold. "What happened to you? You look terrible!"

Harold didn't speak.

Paul walked up to Harold and leaned over so his face was very close to Harold's. "Hello! Are you there?"

Harold tried to speak, but that lump came back in his throat. Tears were filling up his eyes. Paul stopped smiling.

"Harold, what is it? What's the matter?"

"Paul...I just came from the doctor. I..." He was shaking his head.

"Hey...take it easy! It's gonna be okay. It can't be that bad." Paul kneeled down in front of the sofa. They had known each other for years. They had gone to elementary school together until Harold's Grandmother died. Harold had always lived with her. His parents were killed in a car accident when he was a baby. He never knew them. After Harold's grandmother died, Harold lived in foster homes. Then, when he was 21, he moved out on his own. He moved back into his old neighborhood. He began hanging out with his old pal, Sam Bell. Paul never liked Sam because Sam was always in trouble. But then, when Paul lost his mother and needed a friend, Harold was there. He stayed in bed a week. It was Harold who pulled him out and helped give him the strength to keep on going.

They had helped each other through many tragic times. Paul had helped Harold kick his drug habit two years ago after Sam went to prison. That's how they ended up living together. Harold had lost his apartment and Paul took him in. Paul had given Harold the support and the confidence he needed at that time. They were much more than friends. They were family.

Harold sat up. He looked at Paul. "The doctor ran some tests. I tested positive for HIV. Paul... I'm going to die!"

Paul was stunned. He was speechless. He just stared at Harold. The room was suddenly very quiet. Paul got up off his knees and sat down on the sofa next to Harold.

"AIDS?"

"They do have some treatments for people with HIV. They're experimental at this point, but there is no cure." Harold blew his nose. HIV leads to AIDS. Dr. Canty said that is an advantage for me. At least I don't have

AIDS."

"Wow, man. This IS a tough one!"

"Listen, I've got some food in here cooking. I know you haven't eaten, so come on put some food on your stomach. Then we can think about what to do."

"Ha! How many choices do I have?" When he said that, he looked at the scars on his arms. They were track marks from the needles. "It seems like I have made my choices already." He got up and followed Paul to the kitchen.

"The scars never go away and it's so funny...you never know the real damage if you can't see it right away. I quit doing drugs and cleaned myself up and now, two years later, I'm suffering the consequences." He looked out the window. He never noticed that tree right beside the house before. It was beautiful! "Wow! Life is a trip."

"Eat!" It was an order from Paul. It was such a good feeling to know somebody cared about you. What would he do without Paul? He started fixing a plate for himself. Paul was right. He did need to eat. Lately, he hadn't had any appetite. He had lost about ten pounds in the last two weeks.

"This food looks delicious. What is it?" Harold sat down at the table across from Paul.

"It's goulash. You just throw a lot of stuff in together and bingo! You got goulash. It's quick, it's easy, and it's good. It's one of my favorite dishes."

Harold took a couple of spoonfuls. It stuck in his throat. "I can't eat right now. This is good, but I just can't eat right now. I got to think. I can't believe this is really happening to me. I don't know what to do. I think I'll go and take a nap."

Paul was quiet.

Harold went to his bedroom and closed the door. He lay down. "I'm so tired." In his mind, a vision of him and Sam shootin' up! They had shared a lot. They shared hard times, harder times, and drugs! Sam got arrested and got some time. Harold quit drugs and got a job. The two of them sort of lost contact. Now, Harold wondered how Sam was doing a sudden chill went through Harold just then. What if Sam has HIV too? Harold would have to find him. But first, he was gonna get some sleep.

Mattie Bell

Mattie Bell looked out the window of the bus. Every day she rode that bus to the hospital. Every day she saw the same folks. Everybody was busy trying to find some kind of satisfaction! In the ghetto, you didn't have much else. People had to make themselves some kind of happy. For many, that was drugs. Then, they didn't think so hard about things most of them never was gonna have. For them, a dream was pure foolishness because most of them would never leave the ghetto. Her son was a victim of that hopelessness.

Since he was a young boy of twelve, he had been in and out of trouble. His father went to jail before he was born, not that he woulda been much help anyway. He got killed in there. Women always loved her son, and he loved the streets. He used to say "I can't get nothin' sitting here, Mama." She wanted to send him to private school and to camp the way rich folks did their children to keep them out of trouble, but, there just wasn't ever enough money. She could barely keep food in the house. Sam got to know the streets pretty good!

Mattie never really got a chance to know her son. When he got arrested for armed robbery and murder, she couldn't believe he was capable of such a thing, but he told he did it. Deep down inside she knew he was a good boy; he just never had a chance!

He used to bring her flowers some time. He used to steal them out of somebody's yard before he could buy 'em. He'd come in with his hands behind his back and say "Close your eyes, Mama." Then he'd give them to her and kiss her. "I love you, Mama."

One time she went in his room when he was asleep. He didn't have his arms covered up like he did most of his grown life. She saw those marks all over his arms. She wanted to uncover him and look at his body. "Why, son?" she wanted to ask. She wanted to help him so bad, but she didn't know what to do. She could only cry.

She cried many tears and she knows "and it ain't over yet." They released him from the prison because he was real sick. They said he was gonna die. He got something new that nobody knows too much about. There is no cure for it. The name was so long, she couldn't remember that, she just remembered they called it AIDS. "That's a funny name for something he's gonna die from."

The bus let her out in front of the hospital. All the nurses in the unit were accustomed to seeing Mattie come. She made sure he ate. Some of the attendants were very cruel. They would leave his trays in the hallway and would take them away untouched. She washed his face and brushed his teeth. She helped the nurses change Sam's diapers. He had to wear them now because he had diarrhea all the time and he couldn't control it. He only weighed about ninety pounds. His body was all curled up. He couldn't straighten out his legs any more. He was in constant pain. They had to turn him over to try to keep him from getting more bedsores.

He couldn't even talk anymore, but his eyes let her know he was waiting for her to come every day. She never let him see the pain or her tears. She couldn't let him know that she knew any day now he would leave her forever. "I love you, Sam." She stroked his hair that had completely changed from nappy to baby fine.

Most of her family and friends didn't call anymore. They didn't want to catch this thing. Some even told her to stay away from him. "Stay away from my own son?" How could they even suggest such a thing? She would spend every moment she could with him. "I'm just sorry we starting so late." He would sometimes go to sleep when she came. Mattie thought "It's probably the only peace he knows."

Harold's Dream

"Hey Man." Sam was smiling. "Let's go. They're waiting for us, Man. We'll go on over there and then we'll go to the hospital. They got some clean stuff, man. Don't worry about it."

Harold woke up as he jumped straight up in his bed. He was soaking wet. Was he having a bad dream? He was having chills. He wrapped himself up in the covers.

"I better call Dr. Canty."

He looked at the clock. It was 6:00. He would call his emergency number.

"Doctor's office." The woman answered.

"I need to talk to Dr. Canty right away."

"The office is not open yet, is this an emergency?"

"Yes. Will you page him? My name is Harold Wright."

"What's your phone number, Harold?"

"555-6677."

"I'll page him."

"How long will it take?" Harold was impatient.

"I can't tell you that, Sir, but they usually respond very quickly."

"Thank you." Harold hung up the phone. He stared at it. "Please Dr. Canty. Call me. I don't know what to do." He felt almost paralyzed. He was cold. "I'll make some coffee. He'll call by then." Harold walked with the covers still wrapped around him over to the dresser and got out a pair of socks and put them on. He dressed quickly, putting on a tee-shirt, a shirt, pants and a sweater. The phone rang.

"Harold?" It was Dr. Canty.

"Dr. Canty, I can't go to work, I don't know what to do. I'm so cold..."

"Harold, why don't you meet me at my office at 8 o'clock? We can talk and I can get you started on a treatment program. Okay?"

"Okay. Is it alright if I drink coffee?"

"Eat, drink whatever you like. I'll see you at eight." Harold felt relieved. Maybe he wouldn't die. Maybe they would find a cure for it in time to save him. "Yeah. That's gotta be it. I can't die right now. It's too soon!"

When Harold reached the kitchen, Paul had already made some coffee. He was sitting at the table drinking a cup.

"Good morning." He smiled at Harold.

"Good morning. This coffee smells so good. I was just coming to make some."

"Well, help yourself. How do you feel this morning?"

"Okay, I guess. I had a bad dream and I woke up in a cold sweat. I'm not going to work today. I'm going to see Dr. Canty. He's going to get me started on a treatment program."

"Where's his office?"

"Not that far. It's in the professional building at Mt. Sinai Hospital. I guess the treatment center is in the hospital."

"Well, I got to run." Paul looked at his watch. "I'm going to be early this morning."

"You are really early!" Harold looked at the clock on the wall. It read 6:35. "About an hour early."

"I got a lot of work to catch up on. See you later." He took his jacket off the chair and left. Harold heard the door close. "Now that's what I call dedication!"

The phone rang. He picked it up.

"Hello."

"Hello yourself." Carolyn! Harold hadn't thought about her. He had dated her for a while some time ago. He met her at a party thrown by a mutual friend, Yvonne. Carolyn and Yvonne worked together. It hadn't developed into anything really special, but Carolyn seemed to think more of it than Harold did. However, they stayed in touch until Harold started the tests with Dr. Canty.

"Carolyn, how have you been?" Harold tried to maintain a casual tone.

"I've been fine. I was wondering about you. I haven't heard from you. Is everything okay?"

Harold's mind was racing. What could he tell her? She needed to know. They had been intimate a few times. Should he tell her now or later? On the phone…or in person? In person would probably be best. She was waiting.

"Harold?"

"Carolyn, I have been really sick. In fact, I'm going to the doctor today." He took a deep breath. This is not going to go away. "Carolyn, are you going to be busy this evening? I really need to talk to you."

"Well, I was hoping you would want to see me. I certainly do want to see you." Carolyn was being very sexy. She had no inclination that anything was wrong. Why should she? Who would ever guess such a terrible thing would happen to them. He felt awful that somebody else was affected by his own self-destruction.

"Carolyn, I have some news. It's not good news."

"What is it? What's wrong?"

"I really want to talk in person, but it's important for you to get a physical right away." There was silence at the other end of the phone.

"Harold, you tell me now! What are you talking about? What is wrong?"

"Carolyn, you don't know how terrible I feel to have to tell you this..." Harold felt his voice tremble and tears filled his eyes. "My doctor says..." Harold was sobbing uncontrollably. "I am HIV positive. Carolyn... I'm so sorry!"

He hung up the phone. He threw his cup against the wall with all his might. It broke into pieces. Harold wrapped his arms around his body as he felt that knot in his stomach again. "Oh God! Please don't let her have it. It's not her fault." He fell to his knees and crouched over. The pain was ripping apart his insides. "What am I going to do? Not only have I messed up my life, but now somebody else is suffering because of me. Please God;

please don't let her die because of me. She doesn't deserve that."

The Doctor's Orders

"Come on in, Harold." Dr. Canty held the door open for Harold. Dr. Canty sat down behind his desk. Harold sat across from him. Harold's eyes were puffy and red.

"You're having a rough time, I know. There's a support group for HIV/AIDS patients. I want you to contact them. They are patients themselves and they sort of offer some insight and encouragement to help the patients and their families. It's important that you aren't alone now. You understand?"

"Yeah. You know, Dr. Canty, I had this girlfriend. What are the chances that she has this thing too?"

"Were you intimate with her?"

"Yes."

"Well..." Dr. Canty looked thoughtful. "She should be tested right away. I can't say what her chances are. Some women known to have sexual contact with HIV/AIDS patients have been fortunate. It's not 100 percent either way, but ...did you tell her already?"

"Yes. This morning."

Dr. Canty shook his head. "That probably got your day off to a great start. Well, we can work on making you feel better now. I want you to go over to the treatment center as soon as you leave here. It's on the fifth floor in the main hospital. You will see Dr. Grant. He'll take it from there."

"Will you still be my doctor?"

"I'll still be here if you need to talk, but Dr. Grant is specializing in HIV/AIDS so he will be taking care of you. Don't worry, Harold. He's the best in his field."

"Okay." Harold sat there for a moment.

"Harold, you can't let this thing get you down. You've got to fight with everything you got. I do know that! The patients that give up go very quickly while the ones who refuse to give in to it live a hellofva lot longer and better. You've got to keep living. If you stop, it's over.

You know, just because you're sick, it doesn't mean you're going to die before someone who does have not your problem. Nobody ever knows when their time will come. That includes me. I could walk out of here right now, or stay here, for that matter, and die from a number of things. You keep that in mind. When it comes down to dying, it could be anybody's turn. HIV positive don't mean death! I know it's easy to say that because I don't have it, but if you let it scare you, you're gonna lose. The real challenge is trying to keep you from going into full-blown AIDS. That's one advantage you have. Right now you try to enjoy the time you have left."

Harold sat there silently for a moment. Thank you Dr. Canty. I'll try." He stood up. "Will I be seeing you again?"

"No. Not unless you need to talk to me. I'll be here for you anytime. Dr. Grant will give you the information on that support group. Make sure you contact them. He stood up and extended his hand. Harold shook it. "Take care."

"You too." Harold smiled for the first time today. "Don't you die on me." They laughed. It felt good to laugh.

On the way outside Harold thought, "Maybe Doc was right. Someway, somehow, he would have to find the strength to fight. It was good that he didn't have AIDS yet."

Dr. Grant Checks Harold

"Would you have a seat in the waiting room? Dr. Grant will be right with you."

Harold walked to the waiting room and sat to wait for Dr. Grant. The furniture was very modern and colorful. It was a cheerful room. He picked out a magazine to read.

"Harold?"

Harold was startled. "Yes."

"I'm Dr. Grant." He extended his hand to Harold. They shook. "Come with me, will you?" Harold followed him down the hall and into an examining room. Dr. Grant closed the door.

"I have spoken with Dr. Canty. He's furnished me with all of your test results but I want to do some further testing. I want to admit you for a week or so. How soon can you arrange it?

"Well... I guess right away. I don't have any plans right now."

"Good! I want to get started as soon as possible. Can you come back in the morning about eleven?"

"Sure."

"I will see you then." Dr. Grant started out the door.

"Uh... Dr. Grant, Dr. Canty told me that you could put me in touch with a support group for HIV/AIDS patients."

"I'll make sure they come to you while you're here. Okay?"

"Okay."

"I'll see you tomorrow. And Harold..." Dr. Grant faced him.

"Yes?"

"Don't worry. We're doing everything we can."

"Yeah. See you tomorrow." Harold walked down the hall. Most of the rooms he passed were occupied.

"I wonder which one will be mine." He stopped dead in his tracks. There was a woman in this room. She wasn't a patient. She looked so familiar. She looked at Harold. She was trying to feed the guy in that bed. She didn't recognize Harold. He didn't want to be standing there staring at this lady. Still, her face seemed so familiar. He knew her from someplace! He moved along. Her face stayed in his mind as he drove home.

Dr. Canty's nurse buzzed the private office phone.

"There's a Paul Robinson on the phone. He says it's very important that he speak with you. He says he's Harold Wright's roommate."

Hospital Stay for Harold

Harold hung up the phone. Where could Paul be? Harold had been trying to reach him for two days now. He wasn't at home when Harold went to get his things for his stay in the hospital. It wasn't like Paul to stay away and not let Harold know where he was.

Breakfast! Harold could hear the clatter of the trays down the hall. He was starved! He cleared off a place for his tray. He hadn't eaten for two days. He didn't have an appetite. "One must have an appetite to eat hospital food!" Well, he was hungry enough this morning!

"Mr. Wright?" A young orderly came into Harold's room. He held an envelope in his hand.

"Yes, that's me." Harold was curious.

"This is for you." The orderly gave the envelope to Harold and turned to leave."

Harold recognized the handwriting on the front of the envelope. It was from Paul. There was no postage.

"Thank you." Harold shouted after him. He opened the letter:

>   *Dear Harold,*
>   *I know this is very hard for you to understand this right now,*

but I have to protect myself. I'm sorry this is happening to you. You know I love you. We've been through so much together. I'm sorry mostly because I can't handle this one. I just don't know what else to do.

I put your things in storage for you. The information and the key are with this letter. I will pray for you.
Paul

The woman appeared with Harold's breakfast tray. She was covered from head to toe. She was wearing a mask, a gown, and rubber gloves. She sat the tray in front of him and, without a word, turned around to go.

Harold picked up the tray she had just sat in front of him and hurled it against the wall. She made a quick move to the side. It missed her.

"Why do you work here?" His voice was trembling.

She just stood there looking at him. Finally she turned and walked very briskly out the door.

Harold ran to the door. "If you're so damned scared, why do you work here?" He was trying to yell after her, but the words stuck in his throat. "Oh, Paul. You're all I got left! How could you do this to me?" There was this giant-sized knot wrenching in his stomach. He slid down onto the floor. "Oh God! Please forgive me! Please don't let me die!"

Somewhere in the distance, he heard a woman's voice. "Somebody, help me get Mr. Wright up off the floor."

Harold heard some more voices and then they were lifting him up. They put him back in his bed. They put the rails up on his bed.

"I'll call Dr. Grant." It was the woman's voice again. Harold was totally motionless. There was a big pain that felt like a knot silently wrenching in his gut. Then, suddenly, everybody was gone. Harold lay still. The quiet was one he never heard before. He was so, so tired....

"If you don't eat, you gonna make yourself sick."

Harold woke up with a start. There was somebody leaning over him. She was almost whispering. Her face was close to his. Harold turned to look at her. He pulled his face back to look at her real good. It was the lady he saw in the room down the hall. She looked so familiar to him.

"Who are you?" She was wiping his forehead with a cold washcloth. It sure did feel great.

"My name is Mattie. My son is down the hall. He's real sick now. He don't talk much anymore." She poured some water in a cup. "I heard you throwing that food around down here. I said to myself, "He better eat that food." One thing for sure: If you don't eat, you won't be able to throw nothing else!" She lifted his head. "Here, drink this water."

Harold obeyed her.

"What's your name?" She asked when he finished.

"Harold."

"Well, it's nice to meet you Harold." She extended her hand to him.

He took it. "It's very nice to meet you, Mattie.

Mattie stood there looking at Harold. "You know, you remind me of my son. He's been in here for two and a half months now. They say he won't make it back out again."

"I'm sorry to hear that." It was strange how that made Harold feel better! Somebody was worse off than he! And yet, he felt compassion for her. "You must be having a really hard time dealing with that."

"Not any more. I've learned to accept it. You know, one of those things you cannot change!" She sat the glass down on the table. "I gotta go. I don't like to leave him too long. These nurses around here are not so nice. But you can't let that bother you. They just scared like a whole bunch of folks are about this thing. Harold, you have to keep your strength up. If you don't, you won't have nothin' to fight these aids with. When your food come, you eat it. Now I'm going back down the hall, but I'll be back to see how you doing. Is that okay?"

She smiled at Harold. She was beautiful and warm. He knew her from somewhere. She knew him, too. "I'd like that very much." Harold smiled back at her. She walked to the door. Harold called after her

"Mattie?"

"Yes?" She turned around.

"How did you know I have HIV?"

"Everybody in this unit is in here for that."

"Oh." Harold lay back on his pillow. He thought again about Mattie telling him to drink that water. She gave him a warm feeling. Harold smiled and said"Lord, give her some more strength, too! She's gonna need a lot of it."

Carolyn

"Girl, what is wrong with you? Your eyes look like slits."

Yvonne took some tissues out of the box on the vanity and took a seat on the sofa next to her co-worker and friend, Carolyn.

"Honey, he just can't be worth that many tears!" Yvonne handed Carolyn the tissues. Carolyn took them.

"Thank you." Carolyn could barely get the words out.

"You want to talk about it?" Yvonne and Carolyn talked a lot. They went out occasionally. In fact, it was at one of Yvonne's parties that Carolyn had met Harold.

"Oh Yvonne. I don't know what to do. Harold..." a new wave of tears broke her voice.

"You found out he's married?"

Carolyn shook her head,"No." Carolyn was trying to regain her composure.

"Yvonne was eager to hear the story. "Did he hit you?"

Carolyn shook her head and waved her hand in the air. "No."

"Then what is it, Carolyn? You're gonna have to quit crying and tell me before I bust!"

Carolyn looked at Yvonne. She was known to gossip with the girls sometimes. She made no secret of the fact that she was "nosy"! Yet, she and Carolyn had discussed some pretty personal data and she never heard it repeated. She wondered if she should tell her.

"Yvonne, you have to promise not to tell a soul! I mean NOBODY!"

Yvonne was staring at Carolyn with her mouth open. "This must be some juicy dirt. I love it!" Carolyn was looking at Yvonne intently.

"Yvonne. You have to promise me that you won't discuss this with anybody."

"Okay, okay. I promise. Now will you tell me what's happening? You know I'm your friend. I don't discuss our business with nobody else. So you don't have to worry about that. Okay? Now what's wrong?"

"Carolyn paused and took a deep breath. "Harold is HIV positive."

Yvonne stared at her in disbelief. "Girl, you GOT to be lying." Yvonne turned sideways in her seat as if she couldn't hear before, but know she turned her ear toward Carolyn and looked at her sideways through squinted eyes. "What did you say?"

"Harold is HIV positive. He told me last week."

"AIDS? Did you go to a doctor?"

"Yes."

"And...?"

"He said my tests were negative but I should be tested again in three months. I won't really know until then. Just think..." Carolyn's eyes were watering again.

"Oh Carolyn! You poor thing." Yvonne shook her head slowly. "Listen, I got to get back. You can't keep crying about it. At least you don't have it now. Cheer up!" She stood up, Looked at herself in the mirror and patted her hair. She picked up her purse.

"I'll see you later." She left.

Carolyn wondered if she made a mistake in telling Yvonne about this. She didn't really have anybody else to talk to. She had to trust somebody. She sighed, "I better get back to work." She stood in front of the mirror. "One thing for sure, there ain't nothing I can do right now but wait. What will be will be. Oh, Jesus! What did I do to deserve this?" Carolyn laughed through her tears. "Only time will tell!"

Carolyn walked back to her desk. The office was buzzing with the sound of typewriters. "That's odd," she thought to herself, "Everybody's working." Nobody would look up at her. "Maybe I'm just a little too sensitive. Get to work, Carolyn. This stuff is piling up on you!"

Harold Finds Sam

"**Y**ou sleep?" Mattie's voice woke Harold. Her visits brightened his days. She came regularly throughout the day. They talked about everything. It was as if they knew each other for years. He told her about Paul, about his drug addiction. She was so understanding and so wise. Her son had been in prison. She was carrying some flowers. "I thought these might cheer you up."

Harold was touched. "Nobody ever bought me flowers before. They are beautiful, Mattie."

"I'll go find something to put them in. How are you feeling today?"

"Much better since you came." They exchanged smiles.

"I'll be right back."

Mattie had mentioned once that she wanted Harold to meet her son. But, she must have thought about it because she never mentioned it again. That would be very hard to do. It might be a preview of what was in store for himself. He didn't know if he could take that.

Mattie reappeared with a vase. "I stole this from the kitchen."

She winked her eye at Harold. "I brought some for my son, too." She looked very sad. "I don't think he knows they're there."

One of the nurses came to the door. "Mrs. Bell, I think Sam is trying to call you."

"I'm on my way." She looked at Harold. "Please God, don't let him die." For the first time since Harold met her, there was fear in her face. "I have to go." She ran out of the room.

It was like a bolt of lightning that suddenly hit Harold! The nurse called Mattie Mrs. Bell. She said, "Mrs. Bell, I think Sam is trying to call you." Was it the Sam Harold knew that was down that hall? Mattie had never called him by name. She always said "my son".

Harold hurried out of bed and put on his slippers. "Could it really be my old friend?" Harold took off down the hall. His heart was pounding. "No wonder she looked so familiar." Harold was remembering her face when he and Sam were kids. He got to the room and stopped. "Ready...set..." Harold walked in very slowly. Mattie was leaning over the bed almost exactly the way she was the first time he had seen her at the hospital when he stared at her from the hall.

"Sam?" Tears were streaming down Harold's face. He got closer to the bed. It was Sam! Harold was crying louder. "Sam! It's me...your buddy, Harold. Man, I been looking for you and you been here all along."

Sam's eyes flickered as he looked at Harold. "Aw man!" Sam's words were slurred. His voice was barely audible. It sounded like a groan.

Mattie's mouth was open. Sam hadn't spoken in weeks!

Harold was trying to hug Sam.

"Don't! Mattie yelled. "He hurts when you touch him. He's in constant pain."

Harold looked at Mattie. "I used to call you Mama. Me and Sam..." He broke into tears.

Mattie patted his back. "Now I remember you. You knew my son when he was a little boy. You lived around the corner from us for a long time. Then you moved away.

Sam was curled up like a baby. He looked so different. His hair was so fine. It lay around his face like baby hair. Harold stroked his face. "I love you, Man. I'm sorry this is happening to us. But, HEY! We really had some good times didn't we?"

Mattie looked at Harold. "That's why you both are in here." She turned around and walked out of the room.

Harold looked at Mattie. It was as if she had just stabbed him. "I didn't give it to him!" He yelled. His voice cracked. He turned to Sam. "Hey Man, I never thought this would be the way we'd end up. But I ain't blaming you. We both did what we wanted to do." Harold laughed softly. "We were never real smart, you know!"

It seemed like Sam was trying to say something. It was a struggle for him to talk.

"Sh...! I ain't never been able to get this many words in when we talk." Harold laughed softly. "I'm happy to see you, Sam." He knew Sam was happy, too. "This is incredible! I have been here for a week and a half now. I been wondering how to get in touch with you and here you are...right down the hall from me. I sure have missed you, Man, though I'm not glad we are in this shape."

Mattie came back in the room. Harold turned to face her. He could see she had been crying.

"I'm sorry. It's not your fault Sam is like this. He had his own mind and you had yours. I'm not gonna spend his last days being mad. It's just so...so...." She shook her head and looked down. Then she looked at Harold,"You know, that is the first time he's tried to speak in a long time." She walked over to the bed. "Thank you for coming!" She smiled, and added, "Son."

"Harold's face must have lit up when she said that. "You don't know what it means to me to be here with Sam and you." He leaned closer to Sam, "But you probably need to get some rest now. I'll be back later to look in on you. Be cool. I'll see you later, Mama." He winked his eye at her as he left.

On the way back to his room, Harold was filled with panic. Tears ran down his face. "Constant pain... Am I gonna look like that? Sam looks awful. Not like the old Sam." He stopped in at his door. There was a lady and two men in his room. He walked in.

"You must be Harold." One of the men extended his hand to Harold. Harold shook it.

"That's who I am. Who are you?"

"I am Dave Thurston, and this is Veronica Shane. We're with W.E.L.L., a support group for AIDS patients. We are folks who, because of our own personal experiences with AIDS, have come together to help each other get through the crisis. And, this is Father Geary, the hospital Chaplain."

"How are you feeling today, Harold?" Father Geary wanted to know as he shook Harold's hand.

"Better Father. I'm feeling better."

"I want to say a prayer for you if you'd like that."

"Well, I could certainly use a prayer, Father. I hope you have a direct line to God, because only He can really make me better." Harold lay down on the bed.

"We can certainly try, Harold. We can try."

"And after you pray for me, Father, there are some people down the hall in room 207... they need a prayer, too."

"I'll stop in and see them." He laid his hand on top of Harold's. "Let us bow our heads."

Carolyn's Termination

Carolyn could feel the coolness in the air when she walked into the office. Everybody scattered to his or her respective work places. No more gossip to tell her. No more girl talk in the mornings. They barely mumbled "Good morning" as they passed her. Carolyn suspected that she was the subject of their current event small talk.

"Carolyn"

She looked up to see Mrs. Oliver, the Department Supervisor, standing in the doorway of her office.

"May I see you in my office, please?"

Carolyn stood up. She looked at Yvonne, who had not had anything to say since that day in the restroom when she had told Yvonne that Harold had AIDS. Yvonne looked away. Carolyn proceeded to Mrs. Oliver's office.

"Yes." Carolyn was curious. What could she possibly want with her?

"Carolyn, I really hate that I'm the one who has to tell you this...but, we're having a cut-back and your job is being eliminated." Mrs. Oliver avoided Carolyn's eyes. She handed

Carolyn a pink slip of paper. "You've been a wonderful employee...I'm sorry, Carolyn. As of now, your employ here is terminated."

"Terminated?" Carolyn was shocked. "What do you mean my job is eliminated? There are people here who were hired after me. Shouldn't they be eliminated first? I don't understand... or maybe this has to do with something else."

"I have a job to do, Carolyn. First and foremost, I must always consider the health and safety of this office and the people who must come here to work. Nothing must jeopardize that." She forced herself to look at Carolyn. "I know what you must be going through, but I cannot allow compassion to interfere with my professional obligations here. I'm sorry, but there's really nothing else to discuss." She stood up.

Carolyn looked at her eye to eye. There was a wall that was not to be removed. Carolyn turned around very slowly. "I've worked here eight years, Mrs. Oliver. Now, just like that, I'm fired! I am a human being. I have a life to live. What am I supposed to do?" Carolyn could not hold her tears. She couldn't believe this was happening to her. She turned around to look at Mrs. Oliver who refused to look at her. "You know, there's nothing wrong with me! I don't have AIDS!"

"I'm sorry, Carolyn," Mrs. Oliver's voice was soft but firm.

"Sure you are! Life is tough, right!" Carolyn stormed out of the office. She walked over to Yvonne's desk.

"You told everybody, didn't you? You Bitch! There's nothing wrong with me!" Yvonne stood up. Carolyn was screaming and hitting Yvonne's desk. The guards came quickly to restrain Carolyn. "There's nothing wrong with me!" She was still screaming that as they escorted her out of the building.

Last Visit with a Friend

"Hello, Dr. Grant." Harold greeted the doctor as he came into Harold's room.

"Hello Harold. This is Dr. Kato. Dr. Kato extended his hand to Harold. Harold shook it.

"How are you feeling these days?" Dr. Kato asked.

"Well, I'll feel better when somebody tells me this is all a joke and I'm not going to die." He looked expectantly at the doctors. The doctors looked at each other and, deciding to ignore Harold's weak attempt at humor, Dr. Grant began speaking:

"Harold, we would like to examine one of your lymph nodes a little more extensively."

"Really? What does that mean in laymen's terms?"

"Well," Dr. Grant cleared his throat, "It would require a surgical procedure. We would make a small incision in your chest about here" he pointed to a spot on Harold's chest, "and take one out. The procedure would take about an hour and you'll be back in your bed."

Harold just stared at them.

"Harold," Dr. Kato began, "You know that we're conducting many experiments to find out what we can do to stop the spread of the virus. Since the lymph nodes are directly affected by the virus, maybe, by examining it, we can learn more about it and, ultimately find a way to even slow it down. Wouldn't it be worth a shot?"

"A little incision?" Harold wanted reassurance.

"About this big." Dr. Kato held up his fingers to measure. "Maybe two inches. Okay?'

"Okay." Harold agreed.

"That's a smart decision." Dr. Grant patted Harold's hand. "The nurse will bring in the papers for you to sign. We'll schedule it for tomorrow. Don't worry, just pray it will lead to something big. I'll see you tomorrow."

"I'll speak with you again, Harold." Dr. Kato smiled at Harold. The doctors left the room.

"Yeah, bye." Harold said under his breath. He stared out the window. People were moving around out there. He heard a yell. Down the hall, someone was yelling. "Sam!" He jumped out of bed, put on his slippers and ran down the hall.

"Sam." There were two nurses in his room. One on either side of the bed. They were changing his diaper! Sam was still yelling. They nurses were completely covered just like the one that came in his room that night. One nurse was wiping him when the other said,"Be careful with those bedsores. They have fluid in them."

Harold saw them. He started gagging. The sight of those sores on Sam made Harold nauseous. He had never seen anything like that before in his life. He went back to his room.

"Oh, God! Please don't let me be like that!" Suddenly he knew why Paul was so afraid. He was afraid, too, but he had no choice in the matter. And to think there was no cure! Harold's body heaved with sobs. "I am going to die! Nobody can save me!" Harold's hysterical screams brought the nurses running.

"Get the doctor. I think Mr. Wright needs a sedative." Almost as quickly, they were giving Harold a shot. "Calm down, now. "Relax, Mr. Wright, take it easy."

When Harold woke up it was dark. "I slept the day away. I wish they'd give me enough to sleep through this life!" He lay in the dark thinking about Sam. He felt so sorry for Sam and yet, he was so afraid that it would be him with bedsores, him who would wear diapers and scream out in pain from a mere touch. Still he felt the urge to go see Sam. "I wonder if Mattie came today." He decided to walk down there. "What time is it anyway?" He got up and put on his slippers.

As he got closer to Sam's room he could hear a noise. "Did they put him on a machine?" He went in. No machine. That's Sam's breathing! He was groaning as he was breathing.

Harold leaned over the bed. "You having a rough time, huh Buddy?" He stroked Sam's face. "Mattie been here today?"

Sam looked at Harold for a moment and then his eyes seemed to roll around. "I wish there was something I could do. They want to take out one of my lymph nodes so they can experiment with it. You hang in there, okay. They got to find something to help us."

Sam groaned. It sounded like he said, "I love you." Harold just stood there, in the almost dark room, stroking Sam's hair. He was remembering all the times he and Sam had laughed together, cried together, shot up together. He was remembering everything..."Remember, Man. The time we..."

"Mr. Wright! What are you doing in here this time of night?" The nurse startled him.

"Sam wanted somebody to talk to, so I was talking to him."

"Well, it's past visiting hours. All patients should be in bed. Besides, I brought you some soup. I thought since you missed dinner, you might be hungry." Nancy was the night nurse. She was the nicest nurse in the ward. She wasn't afraid to touch any of them. She washed Harold up and even brushed his teeth. She was very attentive.

"Really. That sure was nice of you. You couldn't get anybody else to eat it, huh?"

"Will you get out of here and let Mr. Bell get some rest? He needs his rest." She covered Sam up and stroked his hair back. "You go to sleep, Mr. Bell. I'll try to keep the nightwalkers out of your room."

She walked with Harold back to his room.

"How is he doing?" Harold asked her.

"Not too good. Sam Bell won't be with us much longer. Dr. Grant says his lungs are filling up with fluid. You hear how he's breathing?"

"You mean sounding like a machine?"

"Yes. That's not a good sign."

"Nancy, tell me. Do all AIDS patient go the same way? I mean do they all follow the same pattern? Like Sam's legs, why can't he straighten them out?"

"Everyone is different, although many of the problems that set in are the same. Some die from the pneumonia, some last a year, some two or three. It depends on their will. If they give up without a fight, they die soon. Some of them are in here several times and still go home. It depends on their will. Eat your soup!"

"What about Sam's legs. Why can't he straighten them out?"

"You know I'm not supposed to be talking about this with you. But, I know it's going to help you to know these things, right?"

"Right."

"Sam hasn't straightened his legs out in over a month or two. His feet started hurting him and then his legs. They just quit working. When he came back in here, they just curled up under him and never straightened out again."

"This is pretty good soup for hospital soup."

"I know. I saved it especially for you cause you are always complaining about this food. See, it ain't so bad."

"Thanks. You know, Nancy, you all right. You one in a bunch." Harold laughed. "Sometimes, I get so pissed; I could really slap the shit out of some of the bitches that work here."

"Yeah. Well don't get yourself so worked up. They gotta make a living, too."

"You know, you're different though. You're sweet. You know how to treat people."

"Yeah, tell my husband that. He's totally unaware." They both laughed. "Look, I gotta go. Eat the soup and get some rest. Hey... you got that surgery in the morning. You really not supposed to eat, but that soup is like broth, it won't hurt you. You didn't eat dinner so it will help keep you from getting sick. I'm going to say a prayer for you and I'll see you tomorrow night. Okay?"

"Goodnight, Nancy."

At 5:00 am, Nancy walked back down the hall. The whole floor was very quiet. Sam's room was quiet, too.

Part II

Mattie woke up suddenly. She sat straight up in her bed. She was soaked with sweat. "Sam." She swung her legs around so that her feet were on the floor. "I must have been dreaming about Sam." She looked at the clock on the table. "5 o'clock in the morning. I might as well get up. I'll go to the hospital early today.

Mattie's Last Visit with Her Son

Mattie reached the hospital about 8:15. She felt something different. Something urgent! She was in a hurry to get to Sam's room. She got off the elevator and turned to the hallway that led to Sam's ward. Dr. Grant and another doctor met her. They were saying something about trying to call her. She really couldn't listen to them right now. Couldn't they see she was in a hurry?

Mattie kept right on walking until she reached Sam's room. She started in and Dr. Grant stepped in front of her!

"Mrs. Bell! You're not listening. I need to speak with you first. We can talk in the waiting room."

Mattie's mind was racing. What was happening? Sam's legs were straight. The curtain was pulled around his bed, but she could see his feet at the bottom of the bed! Sam was dead. That's what the doctor was trying to tell her. Tears were rolling down her face.

"Why didn't you call me at home?" Mattie demanded. She stomped her foot and backed away so they could not grab her arm to lead her down the hall.

"We tried, Mrs. Bell. Your line was busy. It's been busy all morning. We're sorry. Please come with us."

"Oh God! Sam, I wasn't here with you." Mattie fell to her knees. "Oh God! My boy. My boy. He's gone." She was crying and shaking her head.

Two of the nurses came running down the hall. "Come on Mrs. Bell. Let's go down here. You'll be more comfortable."

"No!" She broke away. "I got to go be with Sam right now.

"I'm fine." She stood up. Another nurse offered her some tissues. She took them and blew her nose. "I'm fine. Thanks."

To her surprise, Dr. Grant's eyes were wet. "Well, I know the time is probably not real good to mention this, but I don't see a better time." He stopped walking. "We would like to do an autopsy on Sam. It would help our research to be able to see just how the virus has affected him. It would take only a few hours and it should not interfere with any arrangements you're gonna have to make."

"Well, I don't know.... you mean you want to cut him up?"

"No Ma'am. We won't do that. We just want to take a look at his throat and his lungs. You know, he was having a hard time talking..." Dr. Grant was trying to be honest and sensitive at the same time. It was hard for him, too. He was a doctor first.

"It may help us learn more about the disease. Maybe help somebody in the earlier stages." The other doctor tried to help.

Mattie thought about Harold. She wondered what Sam would say if she had asked him.

"Sam would probably say yes. If there's a chance it would help somebody in the future, maybe save their life, huh?"

"Maybe."

"Okay. I guess it'll be okay."

"Thank you Mrs. Bell. The papers are at the desk along with his release. Please sign them today before you leave. We'll have him ready when the mortician calls for him."

"All right. Now don't carve my boy up. I imagine I'm going to have a hard enough time trying to make him look like himself."

"Don't worry Mrs. Bell. We'll take very good care of your son. You can go in now and see him before they take him from the room."

"Yes. I'll do just that." Mattie turned and walked in the direction of Sam's room.

Sam looked peaceful. "I haven't seen you look so peaceful in months. Thank God you ain't suffering no more." She looked at his legs. "They straightened out your legs." She looked around the room. "I know you're here with me. I love you, Son."

Mattie assumed the position she held for months...leaning over Sam's bed. She stroked his hair as she hummed an old Christian song called "Trying to Make Heaven My Home." It was Sam's favorite song.

Mattie's Peace

Harold was still asleep from the anesthesia when they put him back into his bed. "He's probably going to sleep for a while." The attendant said to the nurse.

"Okay. I just have to start an IV."

Mattie came in. "How is he?"

"I think he's fine. We didn't get any special orders from the doctor. I just have to start this IV. It's always required when a patient has had surgery." She looked up at Mattie.

"You're Mrs. Bell. You know Mr. Wright, too?"

"Yes. He and my son were very good friends. I knew Mr. Wright when he was a young boy."

"I'm sorry about Sam."

"Well, I knew it was going to happen eventually. Actually, it's better that he don't have to suffer no more. Thank God. It's hard watching someone you love suffering like Sam suffered. You look at them every day and there ain't nothing you can do."

"Yes. It's hard to watch when you work here, too."

Mattie was leaning over Harold's bed. She pulled back the covers a little to look at the patch that covered the incision. "Is he going to be in pain when he wakes up?"

"Probably so, but we'll give him something for pain."

"You keep a close eye on him. I got to go. I'm leaving a little note to tell him I was here. Make sure he gets it, okay?" She laid an envelope on the table next to Harold's bed. "I've got to go make some arrangements for Sam."

"I'll make sure he gets it. Just leave it right there so he'll see it when he wakes up. I'll be back to check on him in a little while." The nurse left the room.

Mattie kissed her fingers and pressed them to Harold's forehead. "May God have mercy on you, Son? I hope your time with this is easier." Mattie left Harold sleeping.

She stopped at the nurses' station and signed the documents. The finality of what she was doing was almost overwhelming. Mattie struggled to retain her composure. She handed the completed documents to the nurse and turned to leave.

"Take care of yourself, Mrs. Bell."

"Thank you. I'll try." She kept her eyes in front of her as she headed for the elevator. "Down, please."

She sat down at the bus stop. Faces that came and went in and out of the hospital, faces of bus drivers that drove her to and from the hospital...had all seemed to have become a part of her life, too. Silently, she said "goodbye" to each and every one, too. As the bus pulled away from the hospital, Mattie felt a strange kind of relief. "Well Son, it's over now".

The bus ride was soothing. It was so quiet. Mattie was oblivious to everything around her. It was as if there had been a great churning and now it suddenly stopped. There was a peace she had not known. She felt relief as if she had been carrying some tremendous weight totally unaware of how heavy it really was until she could put it down!

The phone was ringing when Mattie walked in her door. "Just a minute" she said as if the person on the phone could hear her.

"Hello." She said into the receiver.

"Mattie?" It was Mattie's sister, Gwen.

"Oh hi Gwen." Mattie's voice was not encouraging conversation.

"I was just thinking about you. I was watching this program on TV about HIV/AIDS. Do you wear rubber gloves when you're handling Sam? You know they say you can catch it if it gets in a cut or anything. And you know about kissing..."

"Gwen, I don't feel well right now. I'm going to hang up, okay? And Gwen," Mattie took a long breath to keep her composure, "Don't worry about me...or Sam. It's really not necessary. Sam died today." Mattie hung up the phone. Almost immediately, it began to ring again. Mattie knew it was Gwen. She just sat down in her big chair by the window. She didn't want to talk. She ignored the persistent ringing.

For the past two months, as she had performed mechanically as mothers must. She never imagined she would feel such a sense of emptiness. The phone stopped ringing. The quiet felt good. It was getting dark in the house. Mattie sat there. She didn't want to turn on the lights. She just wanted to sit there. For the first time in her life, it seemed, there was nothing she had to do!

Call for Help

"Paul, I asked you to come because I know you can help him. If he loses his will to live, he could go downhill very quickly. You can't catch AIDS from being in the same room with him, from touching him, not even from sharing a dish or glass with him." Dr. Grant lit a cigarette. He had spoken to Dr. Canty, who explained how Paul had sent Harold the "Dear John" note. "What do you say? Just a visit. You don't have to let him move back into your apartment. I think he would be happy just to know you're trying to deal with it... and him."

"If you don't know much about this disease, how can you be sure I won't catch it?" Paul was standing looking out the window. Now he turned around to look at Dr. Canty. "How can you be so sure?"

"We done enough research to know that the virus must get into your bloodstream to infect the system. The only way that can occur is through sexual contact, when two people directly exchange body fluids; through sharing a hyper dermic needle in which blood of either party may be shot directly into the other's bloodstream; Or if you have open wounds or cuts which would allow the body fluids to enter the body. If none of these things happen, your chances for catching AIDS are next to none."

Paul was listening, but he looked away when his eyes met Dr. Canty's. "I don't know."

"Listen. You lived with him, right? You didn't know he had this until he came and told you, right?" Dr. Canty was desperate.

"Right." Paul answered, but continued to look out the window.

"You ate with him, shared space with him, and did you get tested for AIDS?"

"Yes."

"And...? Dr. Canty was winning.

"Negative." Paul was thinking.

"So, what could be the harm of a visit in his room. You won't have to do anything. It would mean a lot to Harold. Maybe his life!"

"Okay, okay! It's not like I don't care about him."

"I know and I understand your fears. They are legitimate fears shared by many people who are dealing with this. It's only normal to be concerned about catching it. And my duty is not to mislead you or anybody. If you were in a danger zone, I would warn you. Okay?"

"Okay. I'll go. Do you think he'll feel like company tomorrow?"

"I really think he'll be ready today... and, guess what?"

"What?"

"He's right down the hall!"

"Great." Paul's voice was dry. He looked at Dr. Canty, threw up his arms and let out a loud sigh. "Okay. Which way do I go?"

The curtains were pulled around Harold's bed. Paul walked around them. The rails were up on his bed. Harold looked like he was asleep. He had lost weight.

"Harold." Paul spoke softly half hoping he wouldn't answer.

Harold opened his eyes. He was very weak.

"You're too early. I'm not dead yet!"

Paul could only stand there for a moment. "You been catching hell, haven't you, Buddy?"

"Frankly, I never felt better in my life." Harold was very angry. Hot tears rolled down his cheeks. "What did you forget?"

"Harold, I'm sorry. Man, I been scared out of my wits. I didn't know what else to do. But, I came to tell you..." The lump in Paul's throat was making his voice crack, "I love you, Harold."

He made a move toward the bed but he caught himself abruptly. He felt so guilty!

"Sure you do. That's what you do when someone you love gets AIDS! You kick'em out! Just get out of my life. I don't want you to catch it either!"

"Well, Dr. Canty says..."

Harold's eyes shot quickly to Paul's face. "Did he call you?"

"No. I came to him." Paul lied. "You're all I got, too. I can't just walk away. No matter how scared I am, I know you're scared much more." Harold was not looking at Paul. Paul stepped closer and took Harold's hand. "Please, Harold, give me another chance. I just need a little time. Please."

Harold looked at Paul and squeezed his hand. He was in pain. "Get the nurse for me. This thing hurts."

Paul took some tissues off the table and wiped the tears from Harold's face. "Sure thing." He pushed the button for the nurse."

"Paul." Harold was having difficulty talking because of the pain, "It's so good to see you."

Paul leaned over and kissed Harold's face. He was happy and relieved, and still he couldn't help feeling a little afraid. He thought, "I'd better go wash my lips."

The nurse came in. "What can I do for you, Mr. Wright?"

"He needs some pain medicine." Paul felt like he was somehow standing up for Harold.

"I got some waiting for him. I'll be right back." She left.

"Looks like somebody left you a note." Paul picked up the envelope off the table. "Have you seen this?" He held it up so Harold could see it.

"No. Open it." Harold's voice was strained.

Harold opened the envelope. "Want me to read it to you?"

Harold nodded.

Paul took the note out and began reading:

> *Dear Harold:*
> *I came by to see you today but you were just coming back from surgery and were sleeping. I just wanted to say "Hello".*
> *Sam left us today. I know you will miss him. The bright side is that he is in no more pain.*
> *Take care of yourself. Eat your food and save your strength. Remember Harold, you must never give up for all things are possible through God!*
> *With love,*
> *Mattie*

Harold eyes were wide with shock! Sam was dead? He closed his eyes and faced the wall.

Paul was helpless. "Is it Sam Bell?"

Harold nodded. His arms were wrapped around himself. His body jerked with sobs.

The nurse came in. "Is the pain that bad? You're not helping, crying like that."

"He just got some terrible news."

The nurse looked at Paul and then at Harold. "This will make you feel better." Then to

Paul "This will make him sleep."

Harold couldn't stop crying.

"Mr. Wright. I'm going to give you a shot, but you'll have to keep still." Harold tried to make his body still.

"That's better." When she finished, she stroked his leg. "You're gonna feel much better now." She tucked the blanket around him. "It'll be taking over very soon." She left.

"Well, I'm going to let you get some rest, Buddy. I'll call you tomorrow and stop by. Okay?"

Harold was silent. Paul stood there for a second and then he left. "Damn!" He mumbled as the elevator door slid open.

At home, Paul went straight to the bathroom and scrubbed his face, his hands, his mouth and then he took himself a scalding hot shower. He wanted to be sure any traces of Harold...were gone!

Carolyn's Despair

Carolyn lay face up across her bed. Her eyes were swollen from crying. She was staring at the ceiling. The newscaster on the TV was talking about the rising proportions of AIDS victims. She picked up the bottle of pills she had set on the table beside the bed. She sat up. She turned the glass up and drank.

"Scotch soothes the savage beast." She giggled. She was very drunk. She took the top off the pills and put two in her hand. "Come on Carolyn, you can do better than that. Two at a time. Huh!" She shook out a couple more. She put them in her mouth and washed them down with the rest of the scotch in the glass. It was hard to swallow all of them at once, but she got them down. "I'm going to need some more scotch!"

Carolyn stumbled into the den. She took the bottle of scotch back into the bedroom with her. As she refilled her glass, she spilled some onto the table and the floor.

"Carolyn, you're getting sloppy." She drank. "So what? Who cares?" She stood up and looked at herself in the mirror. "Nobody cares about you Carolyn. And now, you had to go out and find you somebody with AIDS." She leaned on the dresser and waved her finger back and forth at the person in the mirror.

"Tsk, tsk, tsk! Your Daddy would say, it's just like you Carolyn. You so stupid!" Her words were slurred. She looked serious. "Mama would say "Take some Valium, Carolyn. You'll feel better." So, it's time for some more." She laughed a drunken laugh again.

Carolyn shook out four more pills. She shook the rest out onto the bed. "Let's see. How many we got here? One..two... She stopped and took the ones in her hand. "Five... ten... fifteen..." She was getting very drowsy. "Oh-oh. Better hurry up and take the rest before you go to sleep. Can't you do anything right, Carolyn?" Her head rolled around. "Of course, I can, but who's ever gonna know it?" She giggled. "Everybody knows when it's too late. The question is...who's gonna care?" She put a bunch of pills in her mouth and washed them down. She lay back on the bed. "I don't care... not me.. not anymore."

Mattie's Big Decision

It had been two days since Mattie had buried Sam. It was a very small affair. Some of the W.E.L.L. members came to the funeral. Otherwise, it was just Mattie and Gwen and a few of the neighbors and friends. Mattie thought most had come out of curiosity. They wanted to know what a person looks like when they die from AIDS. Mattie almost had a closed-casket-funeral so they wouldn't stand over him staring trying to find out.

Sam didn't look much like himself. The funeral director had to stuff his throat. "They cut out his entire throat in the autopsy." He'd said. "I'm not supposed to tell you that." He'd added.

It was hard to find a mortician who would take Sam's body. She had to pay this one four hundred dollars over and above the normal expense he usually charged. "I just want my boy to be put away nice." He told her not to worry.

When Sam's body was ready, he called her to come and give her approval before anybody else would see him. "Notice how soft I left his hands? Most others woulda made'em too hard." It was true. Sam's hands were more flexible and soft. Mattie was sure the mortician was very good at his craft. He didn't know Sam and could only work from the picture Mattie had given him.

Sam's face had changed from the illness.

Mattie was glad Sam didn't look more like himself. This way, it was easier to tell herself that this body was not really Sam. It was the place where Sam's spirit used to live. Now his spirit was free. She was sure he was with her.

The members of W.E.L.L. had been very supportive to Mattie. "You know, you could always join us in helping all those people like yourself and like Sam." They gave her a card. "Think about it. Give yourself some time to recuperate. You've been through a lot. We'll be in touch."

The phone rang. Mattie picked it up.

"Hello." She dreaded answering the phone these days. Sometimes it was somebody who wanted to know about Sam. Once, a neighbor called to find out the symptoms so she could compare them to those her friend's son was having. It was Miss Shane.

"We're having a meeting tomorrow night, Mattie. Won't you come? It's very important that you share your grief with people now. It helps them and it helps you." Mattie really appreciated her concern and she would give the meeting some thought.

"We will have speakers and some of the doctors who are working on the AIDS patients will also attend. We will be serving free coffee and doughnuts. We really do need you, Mattie. Please try. We can arrange transportation if you need it." Mattie smiled. It was nice to be needed. She would attend.

At the meeting, Mattie listened intently as the speaker, a doctor, explained AIDS and the effects. Since the group was a support group for people affected by the horrendous disease, they needed to know what to say. They needed answers.

"People don't die from AIDS, they die from other disorders and afflictions that are permitted to invade the body tissues because the immune system is not functioning. AIDS, Acquired Immune Deficiency Syndrome, is a breakdown of the body's ability to fight off foreign and unwelcome visitors who attack and destroy." That was a clever way of saying it. Mattie had never heard it put quite like that before.

There were children suffering from AIDS. People who had had blood transfusions years ago during surgery or illness were victims of AIDS. Mattie could see that there was a need for her.

She saw Dr. Grant. He saw her and walked over to talk to her.

"How are you Mrs. Bell?"

"I'm making it Dr. Grant. How's Harold Wright?" This was the first time she had thought about Harold since the day Sam died."

"He's doing better than a lot of other people I see."

"When I was there last he had just had surgery. How did it go?"

"Oh he's okay from that. I just think he's getting very despondent. The only friend he has in the world has deserted him. He came by the other day at my request, visited Harold and never came back. He's just too afraid. You know, families are deserting their own for fear of catching AIDS. Sam was very fortunate. Not enough people are."

"Well, they need love, too. How could you leave somebody you love?"

"When people are running scared, they don't think about love."

"How long will Harold be in the hospital?" Mattie asked. "I think I'm going to visit him."

"Well, actually, Harold is ready to be released. He just has nowhere to go. I haven't told him yet, but I'm going to be forced to release him soon. I just don't want to add that to his list."

"Really?"

"Yep. Really." Dr. Grant turned around to face Mattie. "Be careful, Mrs. Bell. Don't get too involved with these patients. They're all going to die, you know. You've just come through it with your son."

"We're all going to die Doctor. And yes, I've just come through it, but isn't that just the point? I came through. Maybe I can help somebody else get through a little easier. Harold was my son's best friend. He needs me. I'm here. I don't have anybody either."

Dr. Grant smiled at her. "Well, just be careful." I admire your spirit, I must say."

"Dr. Grant, do me a favor.≅

AWhat is that?"

"Don't tell Harold he's got to go just yet. I have an idea. I need a couple of days. Can it wait that long?"

"I suppose."

"Good! I'll get back to you." She shook his hand. "Thank you."

For the first time in months, Mattie was happy. She sang and she sang. She was cleaning house! She could finally bring herself to part with some of the old remnants of the past. She brought out special sheets, curtains, dishes - things she had been saving for special times that never happened. She had saved them for years! It seemed that the special time had arrived!

Nurse Nancy Comforts Harold

Harold's room was dark. Nurse Nancy turned on the small light just over Harold's head.

"Sorry to wake you, but I have to change your bandages."

Harold didn't say anything. He just stared.

"How're we doing this evening?" Nancy's voice was soft.

Harold was silent.

"Hey!" She leaned over closer. "You DO remember me, don't you?" She was teasing him.

A tear spilled over from Harold's eye. He was lying there staring. Nancy stopped and looked at Harold. She wanted to cry, too, but what good would that do. She pushed his hair back off his face.

Harold thought, "Now people will be stroking MY hair." He was remembering how he had stroked Sam's hair. The tears were streaming now. Nancy wiped Harold's eyes. It took all she had to resist the tears that wanted to come into her own eyes.

"It's okay. Sometimes crying is good for you. Sometimes it's necessary. It's okay." She continued to stroke.

Harold wanted to talk, but the words wouldn't come out. He wanted to tell her how afraid he was. He wanted to tell her how alone he felt! Maybe she could tell him why Paul had not come back to see him or even call like he said he would. Or why Mattie, the only semblance of a mother he had known in years, had deserted him. What crime did he commit to warrant such punishment? What on earth had he done? Neither Nancy nor anyone else could give him the answers he needed to hear.

"Can I get you something for pain?" Nancy asked him.

Harold shook his head. "Thank you." His voice was scratchy.

"Whew! For a minute there I thought the cat had your tongue!" Her laugh was comforting to Harold.

"It's good to see you." Harold was happy to have somebody care about him. "I've been running a little short on friends these days!"

Nancy held his hand. Her eyes told him she understood.

"I've got to change these bandages." She began to work on his wound. "This may hurt a little. The tape has to come off."

"You know, it's funny. I always thought I was so brave. Not afraid of anything! I only thought about pain as being physical. I now know what real emotional pain is. It makes physical pain seem like candy."

"Yes, I know what you mean. It's real tough sometimes. You got to keep your head to the sky. No matter what, there's always hope." Harold's head snapped around.

"Hope?" Harold couldn't believe his ears. "Hope for what?"

"You know miracles happen every day. Someday there will be a cure for this. You never know. It could happen in time for you."

Harold stared at her. Then he smiled. "You sure are in the right profession."

Nurse Nancy smiled too. "Thank you." She had finished. "Now, that looks so much better. How do you feel?"

"Well...I'll take something for pain now."

She covered him up. "Coming right up." She turned out the light and left.

Harold Is Going Home

"**H**ello." Harold's voice was wry.

"Hello, Son." The sound of Mattie's voice made Harold cry. It caught him totally off guard. "Mattie!"

"You used to call me Mama, remember?"

"Yes, Mama, I remember. How have you been? How did things go..you know...with the funeral and everything?"

"Well, you know, you get through those things as best you can. How are you?"

"I'm holding up. Paul came to see me once. I haven't heard from him since. I guess he couldn't deal with it. I'm holding up."

"You know, I am cleaning this old house up for the first time in years. I can finally get on with my life although I get lonesome for company sometimes. And you know..that's what I been thinking about all day. I'm wondering if I could persuade you to come stay with me. There's plenty of room..."

"I can't ask you to do that..." Harold began.

"You didn't ask me to do that. You didn't ask me to do anything. I asked you to do something...come live with me."

"Is this because you miss Sam?"

"No, Harold. It's not because I miss Sam. Nothing can make me miss Sam any less. He was my only son. But my life has changed because of Sam. He helped me realize how precious life is. I know now how much it means to share your time with others. It's giving that allows us to receive and receiving that allows us to give. It's all God's work. It's what He intended for us to do. But we all are not able. So what do you say?"

"I can't live on you like that."

"Okay. I'll tell you what..." Mattie was talking fast. She was really excited. It was contagious. Harold began to feel it. She really wanted him to move in with her. "You can pay me when you get a job. In the meantime, you can help out around the house when you're able to get up and around. Okay?"

"Okay. It's a deal! I'll ask Dr. Grant when I can leave. I'll tell him I'm ready to go home."

"Yes. Tell him that. Call me and let me know when I can pick you up."

"Yes, Ma'am! I'll call you back." He hung up the phone. For the first time in months, Harold felt loved. Somebody loved him. Somebody was there. He had a friend in the world! He wanted to shout! He wanted to jump up and run! Harold sat there for a second thinking over the conversation he had just had with Mattie. All of a sudden he had hope! He fell down on his knees and cupped his hands in front of his face. "Thank you, Jesus. Only you could have done this! Only you could have sent her to me! Thank you, God!" He stood up, wiped his eyes with the tissues off his table. "Hot dog! Now, I got someplace to call home."

www.ingramcontent.com/pod-product-compliance
Ingram Content Group UK Ltd.
Pitfield, Milton Keynes, MK11 3LW, UK
UKHW021307180426
11947UKWH00015B/1075